Hudson and Snack Time

GW00859599

for Bronte

This is me.

This is Hudson.

Hudson is my new puppy
and my best friend.

Every day I have a snack in the afternoon.

So does Hudson.
Most of the time he is eating
something he shouldn't!

Monday

On Monday I eat a banana.

Hudson eats a bouncy ball!

Hudson eats a cushion!

Wednesday

On Wednesday I eat a pear.

Hudson eats my shoe!

Hudson eats
a tennis racket!

Friday

On Friday I eat an orange.

Hudson eats
the cat's dinner!

Saturday

On Saturday I eat
toast and jam.

Hudson eats
a bunch of flowers!

He can be very naughty,

but he is trying to learn!

Sunday

And on Sunday we sit down together and eat......

A big bowl of ice cream!

Sunday is our favourite day of the week.

I love Hudson.

The End

Collect all 5 books in the
'Hudson and Me' series!

Available to buy at Amazon:
www.amazon.co.uk/com/eu

Hudson and Me
Hudson and Me Playing
Hudson and Me Snacktime
Hudson and Me Exploring
Hudson and Me Bedtime

Visit Hudson's website to see all the books, learn about Hudson,
and download activities for your little ones:

www.hudsonandme.co.uk

17022843R00017

Printed in Great Britain
by Amazon